Put Beginning Readers on the Right Track with
ALL ABOARD READING™

The All Aboard Reading series is especially for beginning readers. Written by noted authors and illustrated in full color, these are books that children really and truly *want* to read—books to excite their imagination, tickle their funny bone, expand their interests, and support their feelings. With three different reading levels, All Aboard Reading lets you choose which books are most appropriate for your children and their growing abilities.

Level 1—for Preschool through First Grade Children
Level 1 books have very few lines per page, very large type, easy words, lots of repetition, and pictures with visual "cues" to help children figure out the words on the page.

Level 2—for First Grade to Third Grade Children
Level 2 books are printed in slightly smaller type than Level 1 books. The stories are more complex, but there is still lots of repetition in the text and many pictures. The sentences are quite simple and are broken up into short lines to make reading easier.

Level 3—for Second Grade through Third Grade Children
Level 3 books have considerably longer texts, use harder words and more complicated sentences.

All Aboard for happy reading!

To my parents,
Joyce & Ted Larson

Credits: pp. 28-29, Neg. No. 35924 Courtesy Department of Library Services, American Museum of Natural History.

ALL
ABOARD
READING™
Level 3
Grades 2-3

THE DINOSAURS OF

JURASSIC PARK™

TM & © 1993 UNIVERSAL CITY STUDIOS, INC. & AMBLIN ENTERTAINMENT, INC.

By Wendy Larson
With photos from the movie
Jurassic Park

Grosset & Dunlap • New York

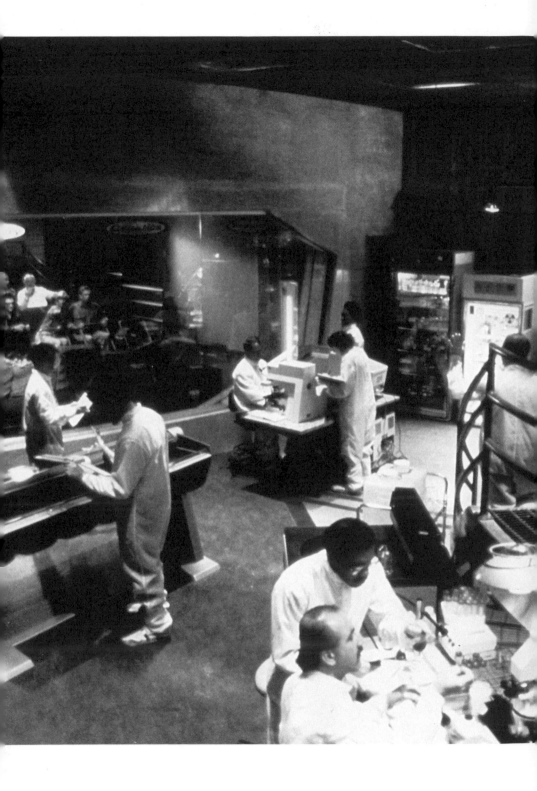

In *Jurassic Park*, dinosaurs come back to life! Brachiosaurs tower above treetops. A Tyrannosaurus rex chases after a Gallimimus. And the "stars" of the movie—the Velociraptors—hunt and kill visitors in the park!

Scientists in Steven Spielberg's movie use dinosaur DNA to re-create six different dinosaurs. DNA is in the cells of all living things. It determines what an animal or plant will look like and be like.

Of course, scientists can't really bring back the dinosaurs using DNA . . . or any other way, for that matter. The last dinosaurs died 65 million years ago—for good. But for over 140 million years before that, these reptiles ruled the earth.

Scientists call the time when the dinosaurs lived the Mesozoic era. (You say it like this: Mez-oh-ZOH-ick.) The Mesozoic era is divided into three smaller

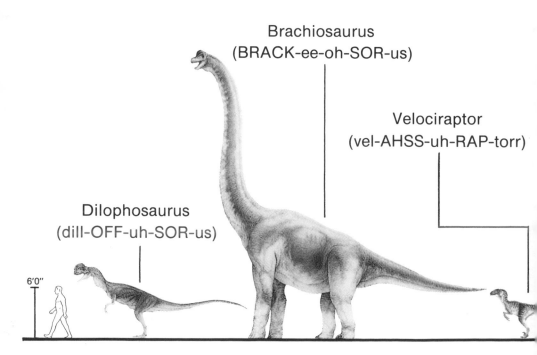

Brachiosaurus
(BRACK-ee-oh-SOR-us)

Velociraptor
(vel-AHSS-uh-RAP-torr)

Dilophosaurus
(dill-OFF-uh-SOR-us)

6'0"

time periods. The first period is called the Triassic. (You say it like this: try-ASS-ick.) And the last period is called the Cretaceous. (You say it like this: krah-TAY-shuss.) The middle period is called the Jurassic. (You say it like this: Jurr-ASS-ick.) That's how the theme park in the movie got its name. The Jurassic period lasted from about 190 million to 130 million years ago. During this time the earth was very warm and wet, just like Isla Nublar, the island in the movie.

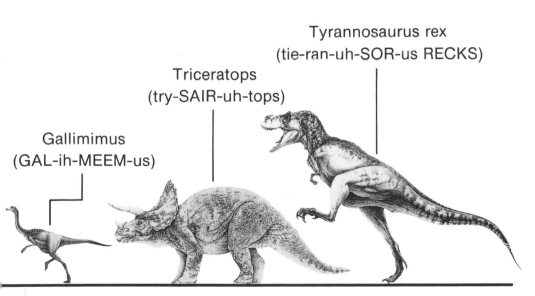

Tyrannosaurus rex
(tie-ran-uh-SOR-us RECKS)

Triceratops
(try-SAIR-uh-tops)

Gallimimus
(GAL-ih-MEEM-us)

Not all of the dinosaurs in the movie really lived during the Jurassic period. Brachiosaurus did. And so did Dilophosaurus. But Triceratops, Tyrannosaurus rex, Gallimimus, and Velociraptor lived millions of years later.

In real life, scientists study fossils to

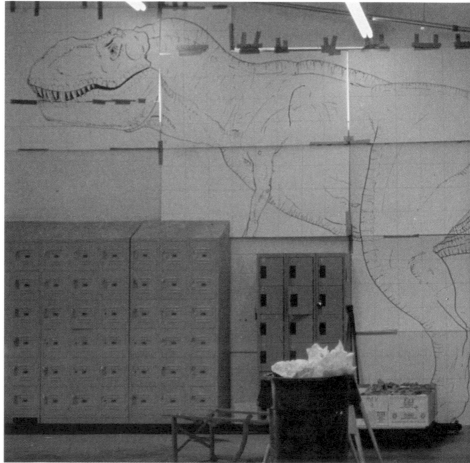

Drawing of T-rex at Stan Winston Studio

learn what the dinosaurs looked like and how they lived. At museums, you can see whole skeletons built from fossils that scientists have found.

Jurassic Park is not real. It is a movie. That's why all of the dinosaurs can appear together. It's like a big dinosaur reunion!

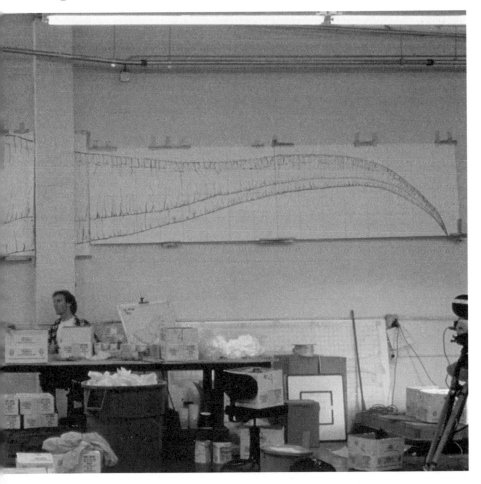

For *Jurassic Park*, special designers—not scientists—created the dinosaurs you see on the screen. They were created at the Stan Winston Studio, outside of Los Angeles.

The Stan Winston Studio has worked on lots of famous movies, like *Aliens, Terminator 1 & 2*, and *Batman Returns*.

Jurassic Park was a very big job for the

studio. Over seventy people there worked on the movie.

For two years, artists drew sketches of the dinosaurs and made small-sized models of them. These models were made of clay. Any changes that still had to be made were made then. Once the designers began to work on a 3,000-pound model, it would be too late.

It was tricky working with clay models. Clay dents easily. So, the designers made plastic copies of them.

The first plastic models were one-sixteenth the size of the movie dinosaurs. Then, the designers made models that were one-fifth the size of the movie dinosaurs.

How did the designers know what the different dinosaurs looked like? They didn't know for sure. No one does. And what we <u>do</u> know about the dinosaur world constantly changes as new discoveries are made. So, the designers made sure to use the most up-to-date scientific information.

Jack Horner, a famous paleontologist, helped the designers. A paleontologist (you say it like this: PAY-lee-on-TAHL-uh-jist) is a scientist who studies dinosaur bones and other fossils. Jack Horner told them what he knew about how dinosaurs moved and behaved.

All of the dinosaurs were difficult to make. But Tyrannosaurus rex was the

hardest. That's because it was so heavy. The model weighed 9,000 pounds.

The designers built steel skeletons for the insides of the dinosaur models. All of the dinosaur skin was made out of foam rubber. Designers use foam rubber because it moves in a very life-like way. It took about one year to build the final movie dinosaurs.

Eight Velociraptors were created for the movie. Each model works in a special way. Some of them have cables. These cables hook up to pulleys inside the model. The cables work like a bicycle brake. Just like you squeeze handlebars to stop a bike, the workers grip hand controls on the cables to make the dinosaurs do things—like open and close their jaws.

Some of the Velociraptors are radio-operated. They work like remote-control cars.

Two of the Velociraptors are people in dinosaur costumes. It was hard work being a Raptor. The costumes were very warm. And the actors in them had to move like real Velociraptors.

What do you think will happen to the dinosaur models created for *Jurassic Park?*

Like real dinosaurs, they'll become extinct! The foam rubber used to make the skin does not last very long. In five years, the rubber will have rotted away. But, like fossils, the metal "skeletons" will last for a very long time.

Velociraptor (you say it like this: vel-AHSS-uh-RAP-torr) is the real "star" of *Jurassic Park.* "Velociraptor" means "fast stealer."

Next to many other dinosaurs, Velociraptor was small. It was about 6 feet tall. And it weighed only about 170 to 200 pounds. That's the same size as a grown man! But it was one of the fastest and fiercest dinosaurs ever. Velociraptor had a long, low head. And lots of small but very sharp teeth. These sharp teeth tell scientists that Velociraptor was a meat-eater.

In *Jurassic Park*, Robert Muldoon, the
game warden, is surrounded by a group of
Velociraptors. With their powerful legs,
they jump and attack him. The
Velociraptors kick and slash Muldoon
with their "secret weapon"—huge
razor-sharp claws.

Velociraptor had four toes on each of its rear feet. But only the second toe had the claw. Long and thin, it was like a giant pocket knife. Whoosh! The claw sliced through the air. No other dinosaur had a claw as big as Velociraptor's.

In 1971, scientists found two dinosaur skeletons. One was from a Velociraptor. And one was from a Protoceratops. The position of the skeletons showed that Velociraptor had died digging its hand claws into Protoceratops. And it used its toe claws to rip into Protoceratops's stomach!

In *Jurassic Park*, Dr. Ellie Sattler is a paleobotanist. (You say it like this: PAY-lee-oh-BAHT-in-ist.) She studies plants that lived during the time of dinosaurs. After the power goes off at Jurassic Park, Ellie goes to a repair shed. She wants to get the power back on. When

the lights come on, what does she see? A Velociraptor! It chases her through the shed, swinging its long tail from side to side. Most likely, this is just how this creature ran after its prey over 60 million years ago. Its long tail helped Velociraptor keep its balance.

Were Velociraptors smart? The ones in *Jurassic Park* are. They are able to remember things. They remember what parts of the fences are electrified. And they track down their victims. They follow Lex and Tim—the grandchildren of the park's owner—into the cafeteria. Lex and Tim try to hide from the Velociraptors.

Scientists do think that real Velociraptors were smart. Their brains were much bigger than many of the other meat-eating dinosaurs. Did they have good memories, too? Could they do what the movie dinosaurs do? It is very unlikely, but impossible to say for sure.

Brachiosaurus (you say it like this: BRACK-ee-oh-SOR-us) is the first dinosaur the visitors see in Jurassic Park. At first, they think its leg is a tree trunk! Good guess, since its legs were as thick as big trees. No human being could have looked a Brachiosaurus in the eye. Its head was almost 40 feet above the ground! Like a giraffe, its shoulders were higher than its hips. So its front legs were much longer than the back ones. It needed strong thick legs to support its huge body.

Brachiosaurus was about 75 to 95 feet long. It weighed between 85 and 110 tons. That's as heavy as fourteen elephants! Not many dinosaurs were heavier than Brachiosaurus.

There is one thing about Brachiosaurus that puzzles scientists. It had two holes above its eyes. What were they for? Scientists once thought that they helped Brachiosaurus breathe. But now they aren't sure. Maybe the holes were used to give off heat and keep Brachiosaurus cool. Or, maybe Brachiosaurus had an extra good sense of smell because of these holes! We may never know.

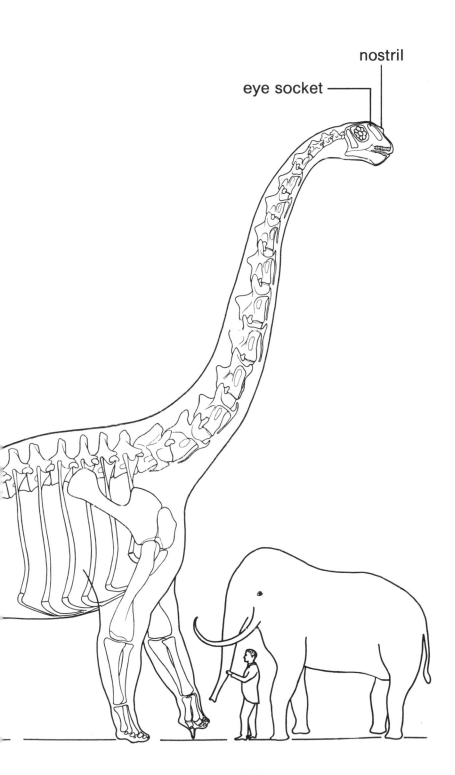

nostril

eye socket

At one point Dr. Alan Grant, the paleontologist, and Tim and Lex are asleep in a tree. Soon they wake up—to see a hungry Brachiosaurus! It pushes its head right through the branches. Like a crane, its long, long neck moves up and down, and left to right. It reaches even the highest branches. Does it hurt them? No. Tim calls it a "veggiesaurus" and he's right! Brachiosaurus only ate plants. All it wants is a little snack.

Dilophosaurus (you say it like this: dill-OFF-uh-SOR-us) was a meat-eating dinosaur. It had a bony crest on each side of its head. That's how it got its name. "Dilophosaurus" means "two-ridged lizard." The crests might have been brightly colored, like the ones in the movie. Perhaps Dilophosaurus used them to attract a mate. But the big colorful frill on the movie dinosaur was created by the designers.

Nedry, the computer expert, wants to steal the secrets of Jurassic Park. When he comes upon Dilophosaurus, he thinks it is playful and friendly. Like a kangaroo, it hops and jumps all around.

Hoot! Hoot! It makes a funny noise. Then, Nedry feels a splat. Something wet and sticky hits him in the face. Dilophosaurus has spit on him. Its spit has poison in it. It makes Nedry go blind.

Did a real Dilophosaurus have poisonous spit? What about that strange hooting sound…did it really do this? The spitting and hooting were made up for the movie. Scientists have no way of knowing if any dinosaur behaved this way.

The Dilophosaurus in *Jurassic Park* was small enough to fit in Nedry's jeep. That means it would have to be a very young one. Full-grown Dilophosaurs were almost 20 feet long. And they weighed about 1,000 pounds!

Of all the dinosaurs in Jurassic Park, Dr. Grant likes Triceratops (you say it like this: try-SAIR-uh-tops) best. "This guy was my number-one favorite when I was a kid!" he says. Triceratops means "three-horned face." A short nose horn and two brow horns came out from its head. And it had a short, bony neck frill that was like a big, ruffly collar.

Triceratops was the largest horned dinosaur ever. It weighed over 5 tons and was about 30 feet long. One-third of its length was its big head! Triceratops used its horns as weapons.

Ellie and Tim find a sick Triceratops in the park. It breathes heavily, and its tongue hangs out of its mouth. What made it so sick? Tim helps solve the mystery. He finds a pile of smooth stones called gastroliths. (You say it like this: GAS-troh-liths.) Gastroliths are rocks that have been in the stomach of a fish or reptile. Some animals have very few teeth.

So, they swallow rocks. The rocks sit in the animal's stomach. They help to grind up food after it is swallowed. The Triceratops has swallowed some poisonous berries along with the stones. And that is what has made it sick.

Triceratops was one of the most dangerous plant-eating dinosaurs. Its only real enemy was Tyrannosaurus rex.

Tyrannosaurus Rex

BOOM. BOOM. BOOM. A loud sound is heard—and felt—in Jurassic Park. It means Tyrannosaurus rex (you say it like this: tie-ran-uh-SOR-us RECKS) is coming! "Tyrannosaurus rex" means "king tyrant lizard." And Tyrannosaurus rex lived up to its name. Tyrannosaurus rex was one of the last dinosaurs to appear on earth. And one of the biggest meat-eaters ever. It was over 40 feet tall, and weighed up to 7 tons!

Tyrannosaurus rex had a big head, with powerful jaws. In *Jurassic Park*, the visitors watch Tyrannosaurus rex swallow a whole goat in seconds.

On a tour of Jurassic Park, Tim and Lex are attacked by T-rex. It's lucky for them that they stay in their tour car. The T-rex is so big that it can't get at them the way a smaller dinosaur could. Maybe size was a problem for a real Tyrannosaurus, too. Smaller dinosaurs may have hidden in places where big Tyrannosaurus couldn't get them.

Tyrannosaurus rex had lots of sharp, jagged teeth. Each was about 7 inches long. Tim, Lex, Grant, and the others see up-close just how sharp and jagged T-rex teeth were. It chews through the steel fences of Jurassic Park!

Of course, a real Tyrannosaurus rex never used its teeth this way. This meat-eating dinosaur used its teeth to stab deeply into its victims. Meat-eaters had no chewing teeth. They swallowed their victims in big gulps.

Tyrannosaurus rex had very tiny front legs. They looked like arms. But these "arms" were so short, they could not even reach its mouth! So there was no way Tyrannosaurus rex used them for eating. Instead, it probably used its front legs to rip and tear at an enemy. Then, Tyrannosaurus rex might have left the wounded victim to die. Later, Tyrannosaurus rex could come back and eat it.

Tyrannosaurus rex could run fast, even though it was so big. Its powerful back legs helped Tyrannosaurus rex move faster than most dinosaurs its size. No Tyrannosaurus footprints have ever been found. But scientists think it may have been able to run at least 15 miles per hour. Maybe even faster!

In the movie, Tyrannosaurus rex attacks a herd of Gallimimus. (You say it like this: GAL-ih-MEEM-us.) Its nickname is the "ostrich" dinosaur. That's because Gallimimus could run like an ostrich. It looked like one too!

The attack happens very quickly. The only way Gallimimus could defend itself against a big dinosaur was to run away… fast!

Gallimimus had no teeth. So how did it eat? It probably used its long, flat snout and beak to dig out food like plant leaves, fruits, seeds, and insects.

We have lots of questions about dinosaurs. We may never know if Dilophosaurus had poisonous spit—or if Velociraptors were as smart as those in *Jurassic Park*. But there is much that we do know. Scientists will continue to study dinosaur bones and fossils. More and more is learned each day about some of the most fascinating creatures to ever walk the earth—the dinosaurs.